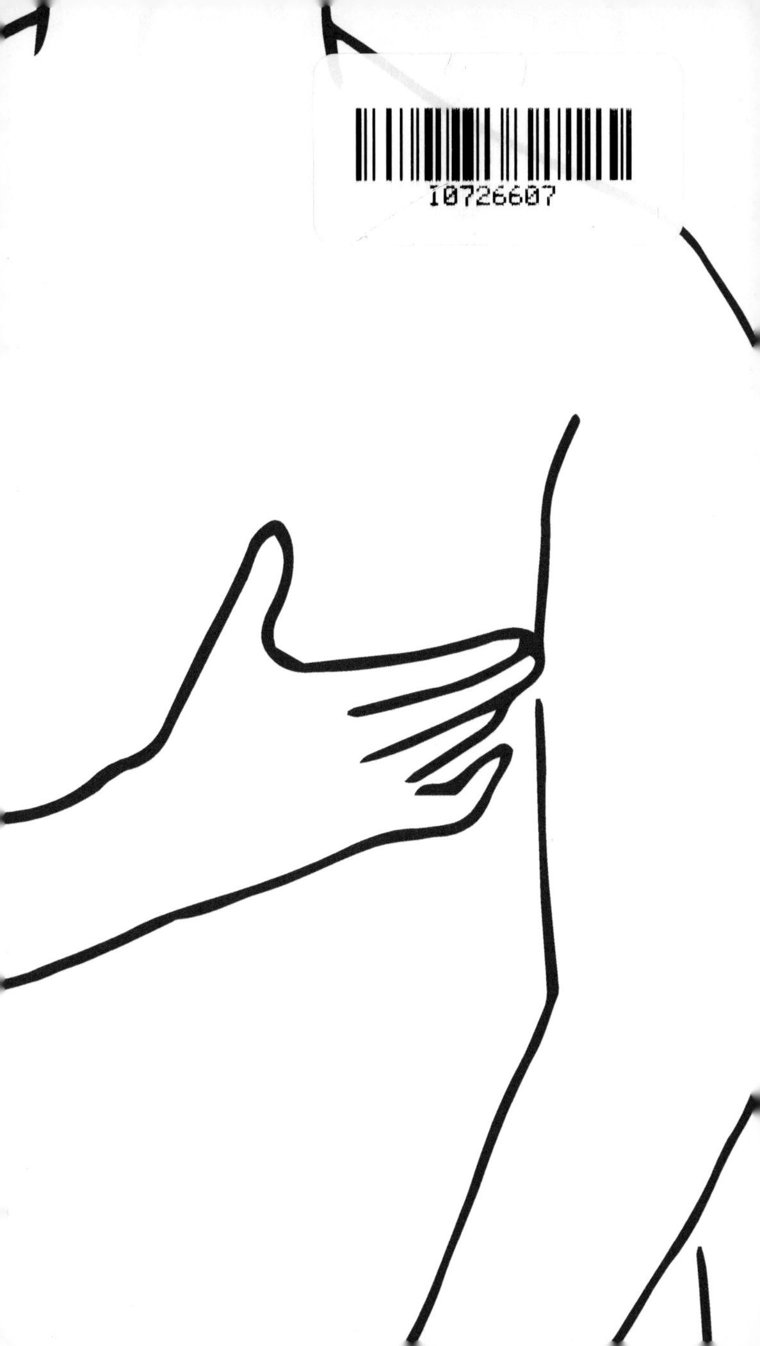

I0726607

girl
thing

girl
thing

stories

morghen
tidd

long day press
chicago

copyright © 2023 morghen tidd
published by long day press
chicago, il 60647
longdaypress.com
@longdaypress

isbn 978-1-950987-36-8 (Paperback Edition)
isbn 978-1-088243-49-7 (eBook Edition)
library of congress control number: 2023944791

cover and layout by joshua bohnsack

printed in the united states of america.
first edition

Contents

ghost of girl

11

the house is beautiful they say

but

bathtub flows over water spilling in drops then steady
stream swallowing the all of the floor around the claw
feet. candle light flickers night drawing down through
the open window blows crisp breeze in the room. listen
carefully crowing of a bird mixes into wind a haunting howl. moon but an idea behind a cloud. water escapes creeps under uneven crack beneath door locked
from the inside. white curtain blown in rippling over
the room in exaggeration. cradled in porcelain lies a
girl submerged and blue. wind screams leaves hit outside the house empty but for her. beautiful whispered
mouths about her once how beautiful. her face a dis-
tortion now swollen water lungs a mouth shaped into
a silenced scream paling lips a hardened o. oh how
beautiful they would say. a leaf through the window
falls in the bath. wind rattles the walls with moaning

cracks candle still flickering bravely. the water of the bath swells relentless in its task.

she rises no drip from the water.

she rises all gray.

...

consumed by house and home the haunted human. melt into walls paper in hands glue sticky gumlike. she does it carefully with skill as if made for the task perpetual becoming she sinking into walls appearing through other sides she who stayed without choice or perhaps. her family here but she's nothing more than refusal denying them sight of her. they who denied her first. hidden she watches them weeping in the living room heads bowed tears wiped more again watching them without pity deep distaste. their bodies distorted through her gaze shadows of faces she once knew. their mourning blacks as if her life a value as if she was more than a face. leaving this she returns to familiar solitude her former room high up in the house that weeps for her. here she weeps silence for herself. water pools around her.

...

the everchanging inside but forever her home the beautiful house. newcomers fooled by the shine they enter again neverending new shadows voices and the like. bags placed in hallways blocked running up then down spiraling stairs she stares from her hidden space watching as she does unnecessary breath held in mouth. away from eyes she waits during time they settle into the house into home. how beautiful they say again and again how beautiful. her room no longer preserved by the come and go of these strangers her room becomes boarded up an extra. too drafty in there they say too many noises they say. always an excuse. the mirror her only remnant dusted over on the wall. they grow weary with days spotless new becomes dust collects settles the house down many nooks crannies difficult to clean a bother as most things. beautiful becomes dull with time they never stay a home a place to linger then leave. she who lives here first she watches just watches eyes porcelain like an old doll. she watches their love die silent.

...

it's not that she minds the company thinking of such

a large house alone lonely in the empty rooms what a waste of space the ways most things are. alone her creaking echoes through the house there are periods when she is alone there are always when she is lonely. entertaining herself forming dustballs between fingers blowing them across the room she passes what seem like centuries but could just be a day or a week with no matter. in her house time works differently she thinks the clocks stick but still tick. spaces of empty she passes moments alone in the dining room remembering thinking of memories here shadows of people who blur in her mind people who have left long ago. how beautiful they say as they pack belongings how beautiful but too much. here she stays her cage her home a beautiful house they all say here the dream of leaving extinguished with dreams of being more than girl. a dream to leave a sentence to stay though cruelty of the world is no surprise to girls. how beautiful they once said of her. from the window in her room framed and flaking she sees the expanse of green something she no longer yearns for.

...

the days moving she does slowly between walls beneath tacky flowered paper she repeats her maze in a daze of days. bare feet above dustballs a glide more than a walk but she is just as much girl as ghost. forever the phase of in between. the house looming takes what she thinks to be days to move all the way through each room her time irrelevant her time worthless. all peepholes and short cuts known to her she knows this house better than any body. how beautiful this house they say without looking far past their noses. dinners in the dining room mechanic fork to mouth bored with their mashed potatoes no butter she watches them from behind the fireplace unlit. revolting lip smacks the clinks of silverware the sounds of being alive. if they looked they might see her but they never do. a house like a second skin caught full of memories of lack of shine. knowing where to hide the presence of her while still being present a quick turn away. the ever changing they comment on noise but never sight of her. the ever changing they say how beautiful without knowing the house. a face unnoticed she is nothing more than another creak. one with the mice a beast out of sight. even mice pay no heed to her a walk through walked over thing not even in the way. in the walls she watches them a child playing with plush toy parents sipping tea. but a blink passes she watches them dying fragility forced by age. a blink she wonders if they'll stay but they have already gone. she looks at her arms outstretched but the limbs do not fade.

. . .

maybe she's lonely the way all girls are.

maybe she watches the current occupants from afar from around the corner. she watches the children play with little dolls with building sets. she watches a girl around her once age cry loudly alone in a room. maybe she watches a young man play a piano during nights. maybe she feels something for this man. maybe she feels less alone during these nights. she tries to sing to his tune. instead of a voice all that leaves her mouth is water. maybe her voice is but a leak. maybe she screams. more water falls from her open mouth silent in its spill. maybe she flees from the room. in flight maybe she returns to that bathroom. this is the first time since the last time. maybe she is afraid. maybe she is furious. maybe she throws the glass soap bowl. it hits the window. maybe this feels good. destruction better than a piano tune. she throws the shampoo bottles. she throws the ceramic toothbrush holders. they burst pieces on the floor. she strikes the mirror. there's the reflection of a thousand pieces of the same girl the

same ghost falling. she pulls down the curtains. maybe she screams. shards and water mix onto the floor.
maybe the family's small dog comes into the room. he
barks at her teeth bared and growling. maybe she grabs
him. maybe her hand's around his throat. maybe she
squeezes too hard. his barks cease. maybe she drops
him into the tub. maybe she screams again. or maybe
she cries. maybe the family finds this mess. they can't
explain this mess. maybe they move out.

maybe she's alone again.

...

in her room she rips wallpaper stripping it baring the
mold beneath. pulling long strips top to bottom side
to side. they never come to check on this room this
sound just mice of course just mice. a roulette plays
with each piece reveal herself not reveal herself reveal
herself not reveal herself. maybe she is more lonely
than most stuck in the attic of herself a mad mad girl.
her story a ghost within. she nothing but a haunting she nothing but a girl. how beautiful they say of
the house too blind to see a haunting the ways the
house screams with her. a tune hummed within her
head while she plays fate each piece a flower petal lit-

tered to the floor. reveal herself she mouths with the last piece in hand. water spills from open mouth as her laugh fills the room with silence. wrapping a thin strand around herself she feels less transparent.

· · ·

the house is beautiful they say a mantra lining rooms. they cannot see the happenings within walls more than beautiful the happenings disastrous their home nothing more than a grave for a once beauty. staying in the lower three floors they feel safe boarded up rooms trapping secrets of the house ones no one would tell family dinner guests no one would guess. how beautiful they say but they do not look in the walls they do not listen to the house. how beautiful they say but they do not stay. the house is beautiful. maybe they're not wrong. she listens she watches. the house is beautiful. the house is beautiful.

she appears.

the house is haunted.

girl thing

she is a girl thing.

she is a dreamy thing. when she dreams she's always much taller than she really is. when she dreams the world distorts through her silly eyes. when she dreams she's always holding hands with a dumb beautiful boy. okay the boy's not really dumb but she wishes he was because then he would like her. she's always dreaming day dreaming night dreaming head off in space eyes glossed over dreaming. she's never living in her body. she's either dreaming or she's drinking. dreaming or drunk. sometimes she's doing both. alcohol makes her dreams sad though and dreamy girl's life is sad enough she doesn't need sad dreams. she doesn't want to be sad anymore but she doesn't want to fix it either. she doesn't want anything except for everything. she loves the wanting. most days this dreamy girl goes to her too small room and cries. most days there's a bottle of jack sitting on top of her book shelf. most days she drinks from the bottle. there's a magenta lipstick smear around the bottle's mouth. jack's her favorite boy to kiss with his whiskey bite. jack's her favorite but he's also the only boy who kisses her anymore. she wishes jack would spoon her or maybe even finger-bang her once in a while but jack doesn't have fingers. another one of life's letdowns.

she is an inferior thing. she's not a beautiful girl but she's fuckable. she's even been called memorable once. that made her blush. she's a little bit chunky too. that's from all the alcohol. it's difficult for her to be a not so beautiful girl in love with a beautiful boy. most of her life is difficult. she finds it difficult to leave her bed most of the time. she dreams up a life lying on the flannel sheets. in this dream life she is beautiful and witty enough for her beautiful boy crush. in this dream life she lives in the hustle and bustle of a city. in this dream life she doesn't spend her days dreaming her life away. she's full of jealousy. she doesn't want to be but that doesn't change anything. watching behind the screen of her phone while her friends travel. watching behind the screen of her phone while her ex is now living in panama. watching behind the screen of her phone while everyone else is living everyone else is loving. she thinks about deleting her social media. she doesn't do it but she thinks about it. she's not sure what she would do with all the time that would free up. probably she would waste it. she's good at wasting at getting wasted. she's not good at much else. she picks up her phone and checks her messages. inbox one. a message from her ex's crusty punk friend who's eager to fuck her. her finger hovers over a thread with a beautiful boy. she puts her phone down and picks up jack. oh to have someone who's always there.

she is a romantic thing. a hopelessly romantic thing. she's in love with a boy. she's always in love. when he looks at her she's all heart eye emoji swoon. he's a beautiful boy a bashful boy. when she says she's in love with him it's only in her head. they have never touched. when he smiles at her it feels like her whole body's on fire and her cunt's soaking wet. as in she's afraid to stand up from her seat because there's probably a puddle. as in she would never tell her friends she's in love with him because they would think she's crazy. as in he probably thinks she's crazy. they see each other twice a week. he always sits beside her these two days. he always asks her how she's doing how her day's been like what a dream boat wow. once she sees him unexpectedly while walking and he's all like hey and she spills hot coffee all over herself. she can't fix her bangs because there's coffee in one hand and her phone in the other. she knows she's bright red. he says he wants to tell her something but has forgotten. that means he was thinking of her when she wasn't there. she's dizzy with love. she wipes the corner of her mouth with the side of her coffee hand because she's probably drooling. his brilliant blond hair seems to just glow. he reminds her of a baby deer all wide eyed. but you know like a hot bashful baby deer. he asks her if she's ever read kristeva and she's already ordering the book in her mind. she will do anything to have another thing to talk to him about. as he walks away she wishes she wasn't always in love with beautiful boys. as she walks away she dreams of a scene in which he kisses her with lots of tongue. as they walk away she wonders if he would kiss her even with lipstick on. she knows he probably wouldn't kiss her at all.

she is an excited thing. it's summer hot and she's waiting in a cutesy little coffee shop waiting for a boy. it's not the beautiful bashful boy she's in love with but this one is also beautiful and she's also a little bit in love with him too. it's crazy she thinks how their names all start with the same letter. b is for beautiful. she wishes her name started with a b. she's waiting and waiting for him to show. they were supposed to meet last week but he never showed.

something about how he meant to text her and tell her. something about how something came up. her friends tell her not to make more plans with him but she does because he's a beautiful boy. the barista is watching her since she's sat down without buying anything. she casually checks her phone again and again and again. she sighs and puts her phone in her purse. when he comes in fifteen minutes late with a dashing smile she feels her heart burst with love. he remembered their plans. she frantically fixes her hair and tries to arrange the perfect smile no teeth of course for when he looks at her. his hair looks like he just rolled out of bed but like in a cute way. now that she thinks about it his hair always looks like that. what a beautiful boy. they talk and they laugh and he buys her a coffee wow. she loves his face but she also loves how funny he is. she remembers that time in class when he brought over her paper to her from a pile of pass backs. she loves how kind he is. he says let's go for a walk and she follows him through the little town into the woods. she's like little red riding hood but he's the one with a red beard. his hair isn't red though so she wonders what color his pubes are. she's betting on red. her cute little skirt that has a zipper running up its length isn't made for wooden treks. she doesn't complain. she's already dreaming about their future together like she knows he'll leave here soon they always leave but she's also dreaming about their future. they will live in a city all hustly and bustly. they will go out every night since he's one of the only people she knows who can keep up with her drinking who loves jack like she loves jack. they will be like sid and nancy. they end up in this little shack in the woods like how convenient. he says the most bizarre things. he asks her if a guy would make a good dad based solely on his knowledge of dad jokes and she giggles. he tells her that it's in a guy's instinct to just like stabbing things and she wonders if she's a thing he wants to stab. and when he gets bored of talking he kisses her. and when he kisses her his tongue is out first thing like some type of eager dog all wet and slimy. and when his beard rubs against her skin it scratches all scratchy and itchy and stuff. and when he struggles to undo her bra she gets bored. he kisses all sloppy up and down her neck her lipstick is a magenta smear all over his lips. they don't fuck mostly because she's conscious of her cunt being hairier than his face but also because it just kind of fizzles away like a slow wake up from a dream. they go back to the coffee shop and she can tell the lady there thinks they fucked. she picks a twig out of her hair and tries to discreetly drop it on the floor. he buys her a second coffee wow. she doesn't see him again but he texts her once in a while here and there. sometimes she still dreams of their future how rough and tumbley it would've been. sometimes she wants to take him up on his offer and visit him in his new big city. instead she drinks and dreams about it.

she is a sober thing. this is when she's at her retail job. it's such a bore though. she's stuck tucked behind the fine watch counter. she has keys that unlock the cases and unlock the counter door so she can get out. she's not allowed to leave the tiny area surrounding the counter when she has the keys. her tiny cage. mirrored pillars surround the area and she walks round and round and round smiling a faux smile at the passing people. she tries not to look in the mirrored pillars she doesn't really want to see her not so beautiful face her overgrown haircut. one of her coworkers comes up with his long long hair and long long beard and smiles and asks if she has the watches that need to be sent away all packaged up. she blushes because she masturbated to the idea of him the other night. she doesn't know him well but he looks like a beautiful bad boy whose bed is probably just a mattress on the floor who probably looks at too much daddy dom porn online. she sneaks a peek at his hands and wow he could totally choke her. he's the perfect beautiful bad boy to contrast with her beautiful bashful boy and her beautiful bizarre boy. oh what a collection they would be. oh what if they all loved her. he's not happy with her because she didn't get the watches done in time and now they'll be late and now he'll be bitched at by his boss or something. she's listening to him but she's also remembering her orgasm from the other night. obviously he didn't give it to her but the idea of him did so that's close enough. she smiles at him a not so faux smile and wanders off to fill the orders. that's what she does here dreams wanders fills orders opens cases closes cases and repeat. when someone wants to try on a watch she takes it out and compliments how nice it looks wow. this is because she gets commission. during the lull hours she goes behind the fine jewelry counter and tries on engagement rings. she doubts she'll ever be engaged. she doubts she'll ever be chosen. but she dreams about it. she dreams of her beautiful bashful boy on one knee his big baby blues batting up at her. their wedding would never be a disney scene because she's not beautiful enough but she'd try her best and he'd be beautiful enough for them both really. she feels butterflies in her stomach as she slips on the princess cut diamond. her eyes tear up as she sees how ridiculous the ring looks on her. her fingers are too short too stubby. her nails are every beautician's nightmare. she's a nightmare. she puts the ring back on its holder and it looks beautiful again. she wonders if her touch would destroy her beautiful bashful boy too. everything is more beautiful without her.

she is a lucky thing. her professor puts her in a group project with her beautiful bashful boy. she shows up two hours early to the pub where they're meeting. she doesn't wear a bra she hopes he notices. she gets a steady buzz. the buzz spreads from her head to her cunt when he shows up. how sensational. they discuss lorca they discuss the theory and implications of duende. he's not only beautiful and bashful but also intelligent. what a package. everything he does makes her love him even more if that's even possible. she feels like her heart might burst. she feels like she might die from love right in front of him. she imagines how this would play out how he would weep over her dead body. this makes her wet. they get up and get more drinks. she gets the beer with the highest alcohol proof. as they walk back to their booth she dreams about him touching her hand. she dreams that he would want to touch a thing a girl thing like her. she remembers the ring and hides her hands from his sight. she feels light headed and dumb around him. she feels like he'll never love her. she feels inferior to him. what a crazy thing love is. he talks and she stares at his lips. she wonders what they would feel like. she wonders what they would look like smeared with her lipstick. when he speaks it's like a choir of angels singing. when he bats his big baby deer eyes it's like everything is good in the world like the proletariat has seized the means of production. when he pulls that bashful smile it's like wow. he tells her he's so glad she chose this topic for the project that he didn't know about lorca before this. she beams and makes a note to buy lorca's books for him to borrow. anything for an excuse to talk to him. anything for him. he stays long after the project is completed. probably out of pity because she's oh so sad oh so pathetic. he remembers everything she says too. he listens to all her little dumb girl things babbling about this and about that. he laughs when she makes a self deprecating joke. she's in heaven. she wants to buy him a drink. she wants to do something for him an obligation for the time he has wasted seeing her. a burning desire to give anything to give everything to him to make this last forever. her plus him plus this pub plus forever equals happiness. he's the only thing that makes her happy. except he doesn't want anything from her. except the moment doesn't last forever. except he has to get going he says but he'll see her around he says. he doesn't ask her to text him when she gets home. he doesn't love her. her eyes tear up. she gets another beer.

she is a sad thing. she's sitting at the bar with her kind of friend. it's loud with live music blaring and she can only half hear what her kind of friend is saying. the bartender is a beautiful boy with dark hair and tattooed arms. she smiles at him too much when he serves her again and again and again. she thinks that if she tips him well maybe he'll like her more than her kind of friend. her kind of friend is a beautiful girl. it's difficult to be a not so beautiful girl with a kind of friend who is a beautiful girl. it's always a competition. a silent unwanted competition. her or her? who would he choose? her or her? she masturbated before she got here so she's worried that maybe they can all smell it on her. she showered afterwards but still she's worried. she tries not to touch the free popcorn with the hand she used to masturbate. the music's too loud and not very good. she likes her kind of friend in the way that's half jealousy half admiration. that's her relationship with all girls though. she looks at her kind of friend with her perfect makeup and million mile eyelashes. she opens her front facing camera and looks at her own smudged makeup. she puts her phone down quickly. she zones out of the conversation staring at the beautiful bartender wondering what he does when he's not here when she hears her kind of friend say her beautiful bashful boy's name. her stomach plummets. her kind of friend says she's kind of seeing the beautiful bashful boy that it's just lowkey but you know. oh wow. she wants to cry. her eyes tear up and she orders another drink. she tells her kind of friend that she kind of likes the beautiful bashful boy too. her kind of friend smiles and laughs and says well he's a good kisser. and she smiles and laughs and they both discuss how beautiful and bashful the beautiful bashful boy is. if she had to choose someone to be with the beautiful bashful boy that isn't her she guesses she would choose her kind of friend. she doesn't blame him for choosing her kind of friend. she goes to the bathroom and has a quick cry and fixes her makeup before returning to the bar. she feels inferior. she thinks about death. she smiles at the bartender when he comes by.

she is a lonely thing. she wanders around the downtown part of her small town. it's chilly out but she wears a skirt anyways. she's never dressed correctly. she's never correct. the wind whips up her skirt in front of a group of boys and she's glad she wore her hot panties even though they're the same ones she wore the day before. one of the boys is beautiful holding onto a skateboard and their eyes meet. for a moment she's overwhelmed by love for him but it passes quickly. she's not used to the feeling passing. she's used to drowning in her desire. the beautiful bashful boy killed her love. or at least really maimed it. her love feels like a puppy with kicked in ribs with broken legs and a broken tail. like a forgotten puppy tied and dragged behind a truck here to california. like a puppy all battered and mangled who no one would ever want to adopt to love. like a puppy who'll die at the pound dumped in the dumpster. that is what her love feels like. she thinks she would rather feel everything than feel like this. the emptiness forces her to think about what she hasn't done think about the ways she has wasted her sad little life. she wonders how successful she would be if all the time she spent dreaming of the beautiful bashful boy was put into something productive. love is not productive. love paralyzes her. as she wanders she tries to conjure up the beautiful bashful boy's face in her mind. she hasn't seen him in weeks. all she can conjure is the face of her kind of friend and she feels like she might puke. she thinks about how easy life would be if she was beautiful like her kind of friend. how lovely everything would be. a beautiful face. a beautiful life. a beautiful boy. she left her phone at home so she wouldn't have to be faced with the lack of people texting her. she keeps reaching in her pocket for her phone again and again out of habit. she wants to get rid of her phone but she knows she won't. she's tired of wanting and wanting and wanting. she wanders around. the beautiful bashful boy doesn't use social media so she can't even keep up with him on the down low. she looks at her reflection in the large glass windows. she realizes she's forgotten to brush her hair. she thinks how crazy it is that she exists when there's no one there to see her. she hesitates by her favorite bar but when she sees her friends in there she keeps walking. she follows where her feet take her and ends up back at that little shack the beautiful bizarre boy showed her. it's much less spooky when she's alone. she sits and leans against the structure's wooden walls and listens to the sound of the river rushing. her dreamy head is far up in the clouds. she dreams about new york city. she dreams about running into the beautiful bashful boy someday in the city in a coffee shop or bar. like you know straight from a movie scene. the soundtrack would be a cheesy song something lovey dovey something like two of hearts or you know fuck the pain away. she dreams that he'll realize how much he has missed her all these years. she dreams that by then she will have grown into a beautiful girl thing beautiful enough to be near him. the part of her that's filled with dead butterflies knows better.

she is a girl thing.

confines

there are places like this everywhere
places you enter as a young girl
from which you never return
— louise glück

imagine

the night in spring rain like a tantrum. a room with a television buzzing. a window shaking from thunder. the pizza handmade one slice taken from its middle. the thunder mellowed by the house's own noise. the lightning dimmed by the lamps. there is a guitar untouched with a song on the lips of its strings. the raised step of a fireplace red with interruption of the floor. two chairs sit empty a sham thrown over the cream top of one. the other without a thing. the record player set to go with the needle up hanging over the record. an empty trashcan mesh outside waiting for anything. a living room on a dead end road.

 there is the girl sitting on the futon next to another body one of a guy. on her face anticipation. on her body dread with its past knowledge. a makeshift bow pulls her hair back. the girl is looking at the television screen. the guy is looking at her. his hand is reached out toward her cheek. on her shoulders the weight of expectation. her mouth is lipsticked purple. her hair is dyed with blue a midnight shade. he is ordinary except his hands are nicer than most. the girl is pulling her body in. the girl is folding in on herself.

 the night makes itself known outside of the room. on his lips are desires. there is the weight of the night sinking into the space. the weight of the night sits beside the girl and the guy. he looks at her. he looks expectant. he kisses the girl's cheek a careful distance from her mouth.

imagine

the day seeps through the half cracked window. the day smells warm like trash. there are screams from a couple fighting outside. a car door slams. in the room there are three empty bookshelves. the sunlight flickers on the empty space. there is dust gathering like a coat. on the kitchen table are books and paper scraped with forgotten thoughts. on the kitchen table are crumbs left behind. in the mini refrigerator there are beers and grapes. a scream outside is heavy full of swears of tears. the kitchen faucet drips with consistency.

there is a girl seated at the table. she stares at the blank wall behind the coffee machine. before her is a handful of grapes. the grapes are directly on the table. from her phone ambient music flows out filling the emptiness. a clock ticks as its hands move in slow circles. the girl taps her finger on the table in time with the ticks. the grapes quiver uncomfortably with the thought of rolling off the table. the girl's face is made up with boredom.

the day seems stagnant before her eyes. the screaming outside has stopped suddenly. the air is a reminder of summer's depth. the buzz of a lawn mower interrupts the new silence. the smell of cut grass layers over the smell of trash like a tight hug. outside of her door is the possibility of anything. the girl waits like an empty room.

imagine

the spring that feels more like a summer for the gasp of a moment. there is an ugly metallic sink stained with paints and residue. the murmur of others surrounds the space always a few steps away. the tiled squares shine sterilely reflecting the room from below. there is a microwave and refrigerator stacked like boxes but the room is more hallway than kitchen. where the dishes should be is a package of newly opened cigarettes positioned to hide the name. the shame of the afternoon lingers in dirt around the sink.

there is a girl leaning against the makeshift sideboard. a cigarette kissed purple with lipstick hangs from her mouth. her hand clasps the thin neck of a beer bottle. intensity clings to her skin as her gaze forced blasé meets the guy in front of her. he looks back at her through the filter of a camera's viewfinder. beside him another camera stands still on its tripod in anticipation. between them the smell of unspoken desire. between them shared understanding of desire's falseness. he holds a cigarette between the shutter button and his finger.

 the unwinding exhale of a breeze reveals itself within the small hallway. a breeze that sweeps away with it the heat of desire. a desire that is more of a moment. a desire that is more of a breath. a flash shoots out from one camera hitting the girl. she is frozen in the frame of his design. she drops the cigarette to the floor.

imagine

the night in autumn warm like a summer breeze. a

room white walls blank in anticipation. the window open pulled up and forgotten. the reminders of an old snack crumbled along the windowsill. the reminders of past sex empty condom wrappers carelessly left behind. a bed no frame lifted up by box spring rests pushed against a wall. a bed unmade sheets crumpled adorned with whimsical orange patterns. the shelves coated with thin dust brushed away in book width streaks. a photo on the top shelf a girl in black and white smoking marlboros frozen in her inhale. the two door closet left open clothes half strewed half hanging deliberation. a night light plugged in. a half glass of water on the sill. a half glass of wine deep red on the sill.

there is a girl standing in the room towards the middle. on her face not a smile but a lack. on her body the loose hanging of a sham dress. on her feet exposure of skin. there is a girl standing straight in the room. her arms hang one on each side. her eyes closed outlined in heavy black. her fingers crossed in anticipation. there is a girl standing alone in the room. she is silent. she is still. she is filling the empty space.

the night quiet featherlike in its weight. the window is open still as a thing forgotten is. the girl stands next to the window silent breeze rustling hair. the silence broken by a scream. the scream amplified by nearing urgency. red emergency lights dancing on the walls resemble more rave than tragedy. red emergency lights dancing off the girl's body. rhythm like a song siren wailing like a cry. the girl watches out the window emergency vehicle blocking the street. the girl watches the stretcher and white sheet. a small crowd gathers around the vehicle men and women peeping around. a small crowd pretends to care for a stranger. the girl dances to the wallowing rhythm of the sirens.

imagine

staying season

in which she swims through desire:

later he will leave and she will wait but for now she is here floating pinioned to an obnoxiously red foam noodle. the waves move her up and down and back and forth. watches forward leaning back on the noodle five friends on a yellow raft. sun catches the wandering water down the all of them all. she watches the water surrounding her dripping over them. she watches her own eyes wander over an array of makeshift bottoms. like they didn't know they were going swimming but they did. wet cotton sticks outlines stick out. sun reflects off the waves laughs reflect off the air she feeling the heat of it all all in her black bikini bottoms. wetness and heat the recipe of summer. she gazes they turned and talking the heat of summer in her cheeks while imagined images are outlined clearly. away she looks and then back again the shameful shamelessness and sips of drink fueling her. freckles on bellies. hair trailing into covered spaces of all colors and twists. smiles curved in innocence in prey. pushed front teeth.

bodies just being bodies. the space of two of these bodies she has occupied one once and the other ongoing. fevered embrace of goodbye igniting one summer last summer. seasons have a way of bringing loss back just to let go again. wishing they could stay here like this suspended in the water the summer always wishing they could stay. the sounds of bodies submerging themselves in bodies the endless desire and water.

the once one leaps into the lake disappearing as he did last summer water splashing her in the face. to think once implies more she corrects her thoughts. a moment of heat of contact and then gone. the ongoing one follows him this guilty feeling follows her. they are a happy thing she's not used to being happy not used to being a thing in terms of another an other. to stay in one place and not feel pinioned there. to stay and say here together say flame in throat say shared spit shared bodies words foreign sticky on her tongue.

gaze moves downward through crystal water clear her ghostly toes moving touching nothing.

...

in which she is in his eyes:

reaching summer night slides its heavy hand of humidity across her body and his too. thighs sticking beneath a black skirt she feels her thong plastered to her ass. smiles half moon she likes his teeth not bright white wine stained like hers. they feel new in this moment they are new in this moment. beneath a tree head on his chest she listens to his voice. biting at her legs mosquitos and the little flies the itch in the morning little hives across her skin. the bartender asks them to leave way past closing time and time spills with ease seated across from him. she thinks the park is probably closed too she thinks she could invite him back to hers but doesn't. she wants but doesn't. hands searching for hands touching tentatively lightly as if he thinks as if she thinks one will just be gone in a blink.

later he will tell her that he wrote a poem about this moment. moment of feeling desire spill watery from her mouth invisible in the dark. overflowing and following one another interlacing fingers neither leading walking in unison as if one. a we in earliest formations. into the backseat of his car kissing her nose then both cheeks. a kiss that asks for nothing more that asks for nothing. now he will say he likes just being with her. listening for any hint of lie the sound of a setting trap but there is none to be found. no force or friction in tongue. no oppressive pressing sigh. she is wary like she is prey like too knowing. relaxed in his presence an unexpected find. late or early the digital clock reads 3:37 he with a drive back and places to be in the morning she with an empty apartment outlined in loneliness. reluctant untangling thinking when again.

she leans through the open window

...

in which she waits & waits:

lying across rough sheets flannel in the summer winters too she crumbles chips dill pickle from bag into her mouth. comfort food though little comfort to be found in such things for her. sheets she refuses to wash in his absence she sleeps on his side of the bed his pillow a memory scent of shampoo sweet cologne lingering behind. a reminder of something shared of something to come back to his body's shape pressed into her bed a shape yielding to another shape in its desire. the shadows people leave behind. her home a home made from her loneliness impenetrable walled in with empty wine bottles wheat beers weed. walls uncovered she doesn't want to make a home from a place she'll leave. well soon enough. him gone so visits from no one no one comes into her place. without a roommate with one room only herself. lips purpled with wine she showers blow dries her hair forgetting the time forgetting that her walls shared with another's home. water dripping rolling down her back aware of each drop. naked at the kitchen table curtains drawn all lights on. stands walks around and around the table circling she hums a tune wondering mind wandering to what he's doing states away visiting family. her own near she doesn't have to be here be alone and yet.

sounds from the next over startle her from isolation. she presses her hand against the kitchen wall white stained with splatters and follows the rustling to her door. open she could leave drive away move into a shared space but she doesn't and she won't. clinking of keys the deadbolt slugging alive to allow them free. watching through the peephole's eye sight of them bright jackets and all ready to fight the steady rain. sitting on the rugged floor by the door she listens for footsteps sound of squeaking boots moving into a space. soaked carpet slushed with warmth. mind wondering what summer does elsewhere. how many seasons can one survive. the redheaded kids next door scream. slouching down rug drags across her back why not wait here any good as anywhere.

he'll be back some day but with him gone she can't even picture his face.

…

in which she wanders until lost:

wandering through back streets up down then zigzagging across the narrow sidewalks she alone hands hanging swinging either side. the streets unfamiliar but welcoming she tries to memorize them like words in a quote remember their placement in relation to each other. they blur together as most things do for her and the often feeling of being lost some way or another drips itself over her body. stopping is an option she doesn't take rather would wander lost and alone but close enough she thinks to home that eventually she'll end up at the right place. there are birds singing in the trees a breeze blows the vivid smell of

lilac flowers surround her the weighing feeling of being alone outside of something. summer outside of
here seems like myth. what else but a warm breeze
licking cheeks licking evergreens. she thinks she
could call someone ask them for time for connection
a desire to feel within something. one hand touches
the phone in her pocket but doesn't take it out she
continues her wandering walk steady in her pace as if
she could convince she knows where she's going what
she's doing as long as it's steady.

the sun beats down filtered through oversized sunglasses she removes them blinks then returns them
to her face a way to hide a hideaway from the gaze
of others. what it means to be a girl alone a girl exposed. the downhill sidewalk leads to a dingy little
store across from the river and recognition of a place
finally returns to her not as relief. the way things
stand still in small places the way nothing moves here.
climbing the low rock wall framing the banks of the
river she sits knees curled up under her chin as the
waves sweep by identical in their pattern. to be a part
of something so large just for a moment. imagine her
body swept away by the current. imagine her body
somewhere else. strength of the river has a sound of

its own softening noises from the parking lot and busy roads. she watches.

her phone vibrates in pocket a message from him a hey how's your day pushing a smile across her lips. she looks at his name then turns off her phone. gaze returns to the water the force of its task mesmerizing. a soft sigh and she closes her eyes.

...

in which she desires desire & nothing more:

moving to music swaying this and that all eyes on her or at least so it feels. loud bar floor sticky with spilt drinks her boots take extra long to pick up. one hand clutched on slopping beer downing the all so anxiety flees with inhibition with a desire to be left alone. drunk she is everyone's friend. plaid skirt flows arms waving no rhythm but inside she feels fire outside she feels every eyes. every except eyes she wants but she closes her own dancing. hand grabbed by someone a girl unknown and she lets her body go with it dancing with another body desired and desirable. bodies bump against her boundaries ground into the ground with crowd packed in tight. the sweat of others on her wipes across her face.

a different girl friend of friends grabs her and their bodies touch electric with energy. a few drinks in and she doesn't remember why she was here whose eyes her desire holds for. melting bodies the way that girl sways into her she melting. her whole body wet with desire and sweat her body seething skin on skin. buzzing steady never tipping over to too much she is here in the moment outside of her head. the hot music slips into her ears as the girl slips her hands over hips and pulls grinding crotch to ass bringing her as close as close. this as far as she wants it to go simply so no obligations no crush. body language misread lips close in on her lipstick switching shared. a foot down a mind made no more. she pulls away but still they dance until the music ends.

the girl asks her home and no no no but yes to a walk. hand in hand in the street sidewalk littered with the night's good time she makes conversation to push off the shake in her legs. the walk stops the realization of home was still the destination after the no no politely no. go inside and smile shyly a smile reserved for nerves charms overcomes. the girl's hand rests on exposed thigh skirt slid up vulnerability's hiding spot.

she is reminded always reminded she is prey a thing to be had her body an expectation no matter who the other. value placed in the moment the desire of her without her wanting the desire. refuse drinks accept weed pressed into apple apple pressed into lips. night heavy weighing on shoulders fog surrounding the house her brain.

the girl echoes stay the night chorus of her mouth.

no she echoes pulls out of embrace a trapped fox chewing off her own leg giving up a moment of heat. she leaves into the mist alone three in the morning drunks in the street shouting she cries.

...

in which she suffocates on the past:

fleeing the sweltering cage of her apartment she moves through the back streets the small neighborhood houses looking more familiar than ever her walk more of a slow pace. the town feels as if it's shrinking around her smaller each time. her own room feels the same the tightening of walls his guitar seeming to move on its own accord closer to her bed. the suffocating closeness of things left behind. the buildings brick and old crumbling in places left the deterioration of loneliness touching even them. a home not lived in will give to decay. her body a home an empty house. her body a thing that yearns for more. she thinks of the distance between here and there between here and anywhere following her feet to the crumbling gazebo at the outskirts of a park she drawn to its shade a small cover from the critical gaze of the sun.

within the small building sits the saddest piano most keys stuck at odd angles pulled up like untamed teeth. she rests on its bench and sets her fingers against the mangled mess like he did once earlier this summer before his departure. staring off into the sky she tries to recall the melody shaky in chosen keys that worked his fingers deft in skipping those stuck in place mov- ing things past their broken state but all that is in her ears is the bar music from the past night deep beat- ing drum of desire. pushing down patterns forming a vain attempt to find the song again her fingers un- trained hitting the broken keys thunking down with nothing beautiful ringing out in return. giving up her hands curling into fists she hits them into the piano's mouth again and again breaking a few of the remain- ing keys the scream of it echoing out into the empty park. standing up abruptly the bench falling to its side a dull thud she leaves the gazebo walking towards the river her usual spot a creature stuck into patterns of here.

once there sitting looking into the river the constant movement of water leaving a place never lingering she wonders if it ever longs to stay just for a moment or so if it misses a shore it has embraced and then left behind. she wonders if the river returns to that shore to stay for a summer.

she taps into her phone i miss you here and presses send an outstretched hand over the many miles to him.

...

in which she is a welcome back:

expanding the light the heat summer in an orb slow-ly expanding she revolving around same town same place. silence moves over buildings over fields bars and sidewalks as summer as people shrink away she stays always staying. a relic in town the eternal girl.

she feels expected like always to be there like paper

coffee filters or cupboard spices. knows leaving is soon but perhaps not enough. something always expected her presence or more she tries to deliver it all tries to not be drained. when he comes back sits at her kitchen table as if he never left it all the same in stagnant waiting. staring watching his every move she wants everything his complete though takes what she gets. he makes food something between lunch and dinner noodles sitting across the table from her she stares his fingers nimble with chopsticks. forgets her own meal she stares unblinking in fear he will be gone when she looks over looks away. this is when he asks her if she's okay. of course yes she's fine always fine a forced smile an unblinking stare she thumbs the corner of her eyes wet from his care. not used to care the how are yous of someone close she wants to break from tenderness she wants to scream. he speaks she listens imagining the time when this place is no longer hers. empty rooms then furniture rearranged no blue futon for the living room the curtains green. imagining the time when he sits at a new kitchen table across from someone else a new mouth a different smile the weight of everything settles deep within her stomach. care that she feels always so desperate such despair. eyes meet eyes then calm silent soothing a small smile on his lips when he looks at her. her body a house in flames.

he picks up the dishes rustling her hair kiss on the cheek as he walks by.

...

in which she lives a night:

melting drenched in unexpected rain a city unfamiliar enough to feel newly exciting. they scurry together into a bar sliding into two tall chairs. being away from home she burns with delight an ecstasy short lasting a lifespan of a night. knees turned in towards her they face each other. they are one breath a warm breath. she is spit coating his tongue she is hanging to every second. two hard ciders her mind never made up in time so she copies his orders two hard ciders and a split meal advertised for sharing big enough for two. the drink fuels her burning her borders leaving as vapors she melts into the space the chatter of the room under her skin she feels the whole city in her boots. the noodles arrive too small for both but they laugh together and make it work repetitions of fine and full how about another drink. future settles in her cheeks as she finishes her second glass she wonders about how long things last. this happiness a night and then back a fleeting time.

this is where he asks her if she's okay his ability to read the language of her face uncannily accurate equally frustrating. a head nod and a yes yes of course. the music switches to something she's heard before instantly louder in her ear her head sways along in time slow and fluid. yes yes of course. thoughts of tomorrow flood but she shakes them away the desire paid to remain present. the desire to remain. a squeeze of her thigh light but grounding bringing her back to the bar to the unfamiliar delight.

...

in which she tastes a tenderness:

remaining in bed well into the morning heat already making itself known they lie legs tangled and lazy eyes. morning breath spit swapped in early kisses intimate disgust that comes with time spent encompassing space here shared. she thinks of the before when her bed knew nothing of his body when he was but a face in a room and now mornings rituals of the here of moments the closeness of grasp of being seen the stretching feeling of being a part of something more than self. his fingers absently brush her cheek down her neck and again the tender bite of last night bluing beneath touch. the summer it closing slowly like last call announcing itself with the waning of days growingly unsteady weather a cause for wonder what next. she moves closer skin sticky with the sweat of sleep one arm beneath her and the other across him as if the weight of all could keep him there them together here the whole day. the sounds of awake traffic surrounding her small apartment screams of sirens and urgency of all. he turns towards her tapping her nose with a finger then a kiss closing his eyes as if returning to sleep was a possibility. the possibility of anything seems alive at the start summer's promises wide embrace a never ending summer until it's not. she reaches always searching for his hand some bare skin to rest hers against the warmth a reminder of his presence the fleeting presence of anything of it all.

dreams move through her mind she pictures a perfect place where they could all stay a place of desire remaining desire. the death of it all not a thought. a space to remain a forever summer this summer on repeat endless and engulfing. she thinks of the group of them friends under the summer sun basking in brilliance and the like. the fragility of it all and despite.

knowing there is nothing like this only stagnant moments between movements and bliss. a sigh escapes her and she wanting to crawl within his skin a complete embrace. the slow morning of today a place to hide for awhile she slides her hand beneath his shirt always yearning for closer contact a way to remain. and still the morning slips away.

...

in which she feels a part:

smiling the dark covers evidence of teeth shown wide cheeks double dimpled. she is here they are lying on the stretched net of a trampoline. lying and looking up the stars reveal themselves in confidence their light one and the same. she is here with them her summer friends she feels herself spreading melting in with them seasonal cohesion but perhaps could be more something longer something that stays. staying in place doing everything she can to stay in ways others don't. a friend already left another leaving soon a goodbye with the season fleeing south. they laugh in time with bonfire cracks the clinks of bottles against teeth. they laugh and she thinks of when this will be vanished the laughs an echo in ears a ghost of the wind.

the promise to return visit and the like always feeling more unlikely than anything. they laugh and she cries the dark summer night masking her tears silent trails streaming grin still stretched the salt mixing with beer aftertaste around her lips.

getting up she grabs her camera flash on to capture this. a them that will never leave one she can hold onto tightly without impede. the click the flash brighter than star's light and she falls back in place with them.

...

in which she returns:

flowing reaching through water warmed by an expanse of season. the lake swallows her in immersing neck deep she stands there still in its cover.

enmeshment

the year is lulling through the last cold months of winter and instead of buying an actual warm winter jacket i buy a film camera. but by buy a film camera i mean i think about buying a film camera. a pentax k1000. an old flame tells me to buy a nikon slr fe2. i spend hours on depop and ebay searching the web for the perfect 1997 film camera. one that doesn't show too much wear no fungi in the lens no cracks or weird stickers stuck onto the body. i mean i want a used camera that is at least twenty-two years old and shows no signs of its life before my hands. i mean i want a camera that doesn't look like it's ever had a previous home like it's ever seen another body. i mean i want a camera for myself. i think of polaroids not the cheap blue plastic one that i already have. i think of restored spectras or maybe an sx 70. something that makes me feel like a real photographer. i have no knowledge of how to develop film. a different old flame taught me once or tried to. i was too busy staring at his dimples. or was it his hair? i want a film camera so i can really see myself. i mean really see my body. not through filtered technology that feels too artificial in my hands to be anything. that doesn't have weight like an old camera. i want to see my body as it is. what i mean is i almost buy a film camera but i realize that at my late early twenties it's no longer sexy to be dysphoric about my body. nothing in your late early twenties is sexy if you really think about it. everything thought stays forever at this point.

i know these things.

my therapist tells me that my relationship with my mother is too enmeshed. she tells me i will try to recreate this with everyone i meet until i can understand this enmeshment. she tells me this comes from my ostracization as a child. seated across from me she places one hand over the other when she says enmeshment. she draws two circles overlapped one labeled by my name the other with the word mother. she asks me to draw what i think would represent my mother's and my relationship if we were two circles. i draw the same thing she does. i do this to make her happy. enmeshment has to do with my cancer moon she says. my mother's protectiveness comes from her taurus sun. which happens to be directly on my south node in taurus a sign we knew each other in a past life she says.

my obsessiveness my possessiveness have to do with my stellium in scorpio she says. an unfortunate venus in scorpio. i nod my head. i am too permeable she says i need to learn how to zip myself up zip my emotions within myself she says and not take on other people's. she stands and makes a zipping motion from her legs to her head like being zipped into a large duffle bag. she takes a deep satisfied breath once she has finished. you need to imagine the boundaries she says and they will come into being. i try to imagine the two circles apart. i try to imagine my body with edges.

growing up i think of myself as one of the forgotten items displayed on the lost and found tables in my elementary school halls. the dirty single mitten dried hard with mud. the knit hat that almost levitated off the table with lice. the old sneakers worn through with holes discolored from their grass days. i would stare at the array disgusted and sad part longing to re-unite them with their loss part seeing them as trash. i wasn't a dirty child. i mean i wasn't ever caught picking my nose in class. i mean i had that gap name brand sweater that all the kids had. i mean i was just lonely something that has yet to change. as a child i had few-er friends than fingers on one hand. by fewer friends than fingers on one hand i mean i had three friends over the span of years. i was friends with the boy with adhd too active too annoying for everyone else. we would play in his rice sandbox for hours upstairs from where his mother kept a christmas tree all year round. i was friends with the girl who liked me because i let her boss me around who had a dalmatian that bit her sister's friends. we would do anything she wanted and she stopped being my friend when her cousin liked me more than her. i was friends with the girl who puberty hit like a dump truck at too early an age whose body scared me thinking about what mine would become. whose dad would scream at her when she was mean to her little brother. we would roller skate and jump on her trampoline. we stopped being friends when her grandmother beat her with a wooden spoon in front of me and i cried because i wanted to go home because i was scared. i mean growing up in a small rural town with parents who were not from there is like growing up in a dumpster. i mean no one wants anything to do with you. i ask my mom at my parents' new house sitting at the kitchen table all scratched and painted on from my childhood if my lack of friends was my fault somehow. she says no she says that in preschool i tried to make friends with everyone a girl named lucy in particular who pushed me down and left me out of the girls' group she says i would come home confused and sad she says she wanted to beat up the children who hurt me who made me cry who teased me about my bucked front teeth who left me to sit alone at lunches. she laughs and says not really but she says she wanted to do something and there was nothing to be done she says she just kept telling me to be nice and maybe they would come around. my mother looks at me with what looks like regret. she says she wishes she had told me to be mean.

when i am young my mother keeps me at her side like a lucky clover. wherever she is i am not far behind. grocery store trips with me clutching the cart's rungs getting in the way of turns. i would never ask for anything i wasn't offered. and even then sometimes i would refuse. to learn at an early age to want nothing. i think i was afraid to seem too needy. what i mean is i think i was afraid to be refused. what i mean is how easy i grew into this pattern of desire's lack. before my sisters are born it's just my mother and me my father always working away my brother off on trips with our grandparents. trips i was never invited on. my mother and i would go on long car trips with her making up stories to keep me entertained with her telling me stories about her life. my mother had me when she was twenty two newly married. my mother almost lost her pregnancy with me because of ignorant doctors the medicine she had to take to prevent early labor. how she moved to a town away from her family away from her friends. i mean in this time i became my mother's best friend. growing up without any sisters with brothers whose ages ranged far from her own she tells me stories about her loneliness about her mother working always about babysitters and nights alone. growing up in the low income housing project she tells me stories about fighting people in school about her friend dying in a car crash at fifteen about being stalked by a man who later murdered her classmate. she tells me about the fears of childhood about not wanting me to ever want like she did to ever fear like she did.

my therapist asks me when was the first time i remember restricting my eating. i sit on her couch stress ball in one hand pressing thumb indents into it. thinking back to when i became aware of my body as a thing aware of the value of a disciplined body. i tell her about fifth grade gymnastics and feeling my body was bigger than the others in skin tight spandex. i tell her in sixth grade i skipped lunch on school days no one ever asking why my lunch bill never came. i tell her in eighth grade i began switching meals with zero calorie energy drinks a lasting habit. she scribbles something down quickly on her legal notepad. she tells me about what a healthy meal consists of she tells me in detail what she ate today she looks to the ceiling and makes a mmm sound when she mentions her apple crisp dessert. she tells me that my libra sun will always make me obsessed with beauty that there is not much to be done about that. she tells me that real beauty comes from within she makes a waving motion from her stomach to her face when she says this. she asks me what i've eaten today and i shrug my shoulders i tell her i haven't yet instead of saying i drank an energy drink and a cup of coffee and called that a meal. she takes out a piece of paper she writes down a recipe for me she tells me it's vegan so i should like it. she tells me i need to grow into my cancer moon that cancer moons love cooking so i should try to cook that i need to learn to nurture myself instead of depending on others that i can find this nurturement through food. good food she emphasizes with a clap of her hands. i think about the time my nana told me i was smaller than my mother ever was my mother within earshot. i think about my mother recalling stories of her stepfather and brothers telling her she was getting fat like her mother. the familial policing of bodies by other bodies. my mother tells me once that she thinks nana gained weight so my mother's real father would leave her alone. he didn't like big women she tells me. my nana's early stomach stapling surgery that made her sick that gave her an early death. i picture a stomach riddled with staples the solution to limiting hunger. the hunger stories. the shame of tightening pants. the way i still keep all of my too small clothes in case i ever can fit into them again like souvenirs. my therapist asks me where do i think this all came from. i think of watching the waves of my younger sisters' weights noticing the spans of fluctuation. i think of the shame i felt for them then the shame i felt for feeling that way. my therapist asks me if i want to be better. i tell her i think so. i mean i tell her i think so but what i mean is i'm not sure if i can if it's an option. she asks me if anyone in my family has ever shown concern about my eating habits about my weight. she asks me if i have ever talked to my family about my eating habits. she asks me if i have admitted to myself i have a problem.

i often ignore hunger screams the pangs and weird grumbles until i am reeling dizzy and nauseous. this is the aftermath of an eating disorder. i mean disordered eating. i mean the forever –ing of recovering never recovered. i look at photos of myself from then. the photos are all deleted from my phone so i can't access them with ease but they're saved on my laptop so i can still see them if i try. today i try. my stomach rumbles with the sun setting my room illuminated by artificial lights laptop screen and the flashing of my phone. the photo of then with my faux fur hat in a craft store's teal mirror my cheeks almost sunk a face too fleshy by birth for true gauntness. my birdlike hand claws grips around my then phone. my eyes so heavily outlined they look shut in black. eyebrows waxed and a magentaed mouth blasé neither smiling nor frowning. a body neither here nor there. the photo from then dated three days after my first relationship ended. i don't remember how i left the house i only remember it being through my mother's begging and promises. promises of a new comforter set fresh orange boxed sheets of any clothes i wanted of jewelry parts and art pieces. she promised me a pug puppy if i wanted one still the one with forever fat rolls and a squished in face the one that snores like me when it sleeps. anything to lure me from what he would call my hunger strikes my cocooned naps of days. in a photo i'm trying on to buy a zig zagged white and black bathing suit. my head looks like a bobble toy too big for its body. my thighs gap enough it seems like someone could stick their head through when my feet are touching. bad home cut bangs my hair long but falling out. i remember when i stepped out to get my mother's opinion on the bikini she made another promise. for graduation i'll buy you a boob job she said. a half joke at best. i know i could have gotten anything i wanted in that moment. the things we do to cover up our mirrors to find order in disorder.

when i move out of my parents' home it's a muddy spring and my then best friend helps me look for apartments. one bedrooms and studios something small something that won't be shared with another. the choice to live alone is less of a choice and more of a fact that no one i know wants to live with me to share my space. the landlord to one of the apartments thinks we're a couple is it the two of you moving in she asks us pointing a finger at each of us. i say no and my then best friend laughs. my then best friend draws the layouts of all the viewed apartments and helps me choose one the best one. i mean my then best friend as in my best friend for years who i used to be able to call at any time of night who ate takeout with me on the kitchen floor who took in my great grandmother's cat when she had to go into a nursing home is also the same person who will stop replying to any of my messages one day. i mean my best friend ghosts me. i mean i'm not surprised. i don't mean that it doesn't hurt. my apartment is small and when i get the keys to it i cry in the empty living room. when i move out of my parents' house i have rarely stayed home alone overnight before. when i move into my apartment my mother comes over to cook me meals. she says she's worried that she never taught me to cook she laughs that i might burn down my apartment if i try. the first night she makes small personal pizzas with no cheese with cut up apples and artichoke hearts. my mother and i sit at my small table with a scar carved into it a gift from an old classmate who moved away. my mother tells me that she was worried about the safety of my apartment that she feels better now she knows the police department is nearby that she knows families live in the building. i tell her the police don't make me feel any safer and she laughs and we push our slices of pizza around the large fiestaware plates. she tells me that she asked my neighbor why they had security cameras in their windows she tells me they said their cars were broken into. she tells me that i can come back home anytime just a thirty minute drive away that i don't need to call ahead of time or anything just to come back home. what she means is that she misses me already. what i mean is i miss her already. my small table wobbles when i reach for my dollar store wine glass and she does the same.

my therapist asks me to bring in photos of me from my childhood. she says she wants to look at my face in them she says she can tell a lot from a face. we spend the greater part of my session looking through these photos. photos mostly taken by my mother always hiding behind the camera never wanting to be in its path. there are a few my father i assume took of me and my mother. in most she's scowling her permed hair an eighties dream loose highwaisted jeans jogger sweatpants and i'm always laughing a child's uncontained smile. what i mean is that i hadn't realized my teeth were bucked yet that i hadn't learned to be ashamed. my favorite of these photos is the one of me on a hard plastic blue teeter totterlike toy one they probably don't make anymore because so many kids knocked their front teeth out on them with bare feet a sunhat and a bright pink shirt which i never would wear now. my mother is crouched down beside me with a hand on my back steadying me. we both are smiling. what i mean is we both look happy. what i mean is it's hard for me to look at these photos. my therapist hands me another photo of myself in preschool a class picture everyone sitting with their legs crossed perfectly straight and me in the middle legs straight out neck tilted up with a grimacing smile. she points to me taps little photo me with her finger and asks what would you say to younger you if you could. i think of all the pain that version of me has yet to go through. i think of every abandonment every loss she's yet to face. i think of the foodless days the days spent lying in bed the days she is yet to waste. i think of all the times i've thought of myself as monstrous hideous taking up too much space. i think of all the things i never thought i deserved i think of all the things i still don't think i deserve. i think of the pain of being a girl. i cry and look away from the photo. my therapist repeats what would you say to younger you if you could. i say i would tell her i'm sorry.

in the summers my mother and i map out hours sequences of second hand stores and flea markets. what i mean is my mother and i stop at these places down the state's long back routes while on our way to the mall. she likes the flea markets because she sees things that her great grandmother used to have. we are sweaty and over caffeinated as we poke our ways through the dusty belongings of old people some things interesting some things actual trash. i look for books for dusty eighties records for my perfect film camera. i look for mary jane shoes for the perfect plaid pants. my mother talks to everyone so often we drift apart during our exploring. silently i walk from tent to tent hiding behind the largest round sunglasses i could find i touch every camera i see. i press my index finger into the lenses. i press the viewfinders up to my sunglasses and shut one eye but can't see anything. there is a time at a flea market where two old ladies tease me for my shorts being too short for my then blue hair and my then pierced lip they say something about it's a shame because what a pretty face. they say this without knowing they are standing next to my mother. my taurus mother with an anger like a bull's she rips into them her voice carrying over across the flea market where i hear from another tent. we leave shortly after she tells me how they turned ghost white i say i don't know how they didn't see our resemblance. we are the same height stupidly straight hair slightly pigged noses except my eyes are blue where hers are brown. i think about the time she shut down the woman in forever 21's dressing room for calling my dress a shirt her raised voice saying it's whatever the fuck she wants it to be why don't you mind your own business. i admire the way her anger shoots outwards her fiery bursts a mother's wrath. what i mean is i wish my anger didn't seethe inside that i didn't bottle it up that i didn't direct it on myself. what i mean is i wish my mother defended herself the way she defends me. what i mean is i wish her mother had defended her at all.

when i dream of home it's always in my parents' first house my childhood home even though i haven't lived there for seven years now. the small ranch house first red and then vinyled over white. the seventies style mustard yellow tile squares through the kitchen and narrow hallway. a storm door with bullet holes from when the house belonged to the local drug dealer. the old grover house people would call it with a sneer oh you live in the old grover house. i would trace my finger over the holes while peeking out the door waiting for the bus hours spent like that. my small kitchen set filled with water so i could pretend i was doing dishes with my mother. my mother always hated the house. i mean my mother always hated the town. in my dreams i am always in the hallway wooden paneling the vent in the middle of the floor. in one dream there is a sweater floating at the end of the hallway dream me is startled and when the sweater notices it drops to the floor. i never go through the rest of the house. the mostly unfinished basement where my father used to hang skinned muskrats beavers otters and mink when the fur trade was a source of money when my family was young. i mean when my family was in need of money. the smell of the tanned hides. i would go with him to check his traps as a young child i would watch him skin and stretch the carcasses of the unlucky animals. raccoons from his hunts with our old plott hound who would bellow when any animal came near our house. we had a toy room in the finished part of the cellar but i would never go by myself. what i mean is i wouldn't go without my brother or my mother. what i mean is my brother was always gone. standing on the top of the stairs peering over the handrail at the hanging inside out bodies i was afraid to be alone with them. i can still smell the dead flesh. what i mean is i don't eat meat anymore. there was a graveyard directly across the street from our front yard. my brother and i would walk through it reading the names on the stones. i mean we would try to our mother never taught us how to sound out words. she didn't believe in it. the kids on the bus would always ask if that scared me if i ever saw ghosts. no i would say i never saw any ghosts.

acknowledgments

Thanks to Joshua Bohnsack, Joe Demes, and Nathan Stormer at Long Day Press for seeing the light in these little stories and helping put them out in the world.

To the publications that have published previous versions of some of these stories: *Heavy Feather Review*, *Old Pal Magazine*, *Unfortunately Literary Magazine*, and *Squawk Back*.

To Greg Howard for assisting me with this manuscript in all of its forms, encouraging my various and always untitled projects I brought to workshops, introducing me to the literature that shaped my writing, and always reminding me that have something of my own to contribute to the literary conversations that I love.

Thanks to my parents for always encouraging me to pursue my desires wherever they have led me, for always nourishing my imagination and creativity, and for the unconditional support and endless love.

To Andy for every encouragement and every tenderness.

To all the green girls.

Morghen Tidd holds an MA in English from the University of Maine, where she was the Ulrich Wicks Teaching Assistant. She is a former-teacher-turned-bartender-turned-grant-writer and lives in Maine with her two parrots and partner. This is her first book.

Long Day Press

New & Forthcoming Titles

An Atavic Fear of Hailstorms
João Reis
N o v e l l a
ISBN: 9781950987290 • $14

I Will Teach You Retribution
Timothy Moore
S t o r i e s
ISBN: 9781950987375 • $14

Sex With My Family
Jessica Anne
F i c t i o n s
ISBN: 9781950987306 • $14

Memory Field
Eric Tyler Benick
T r a v e l s
ISBN: TK • $14

LongDayPress.com   @LongDayPress

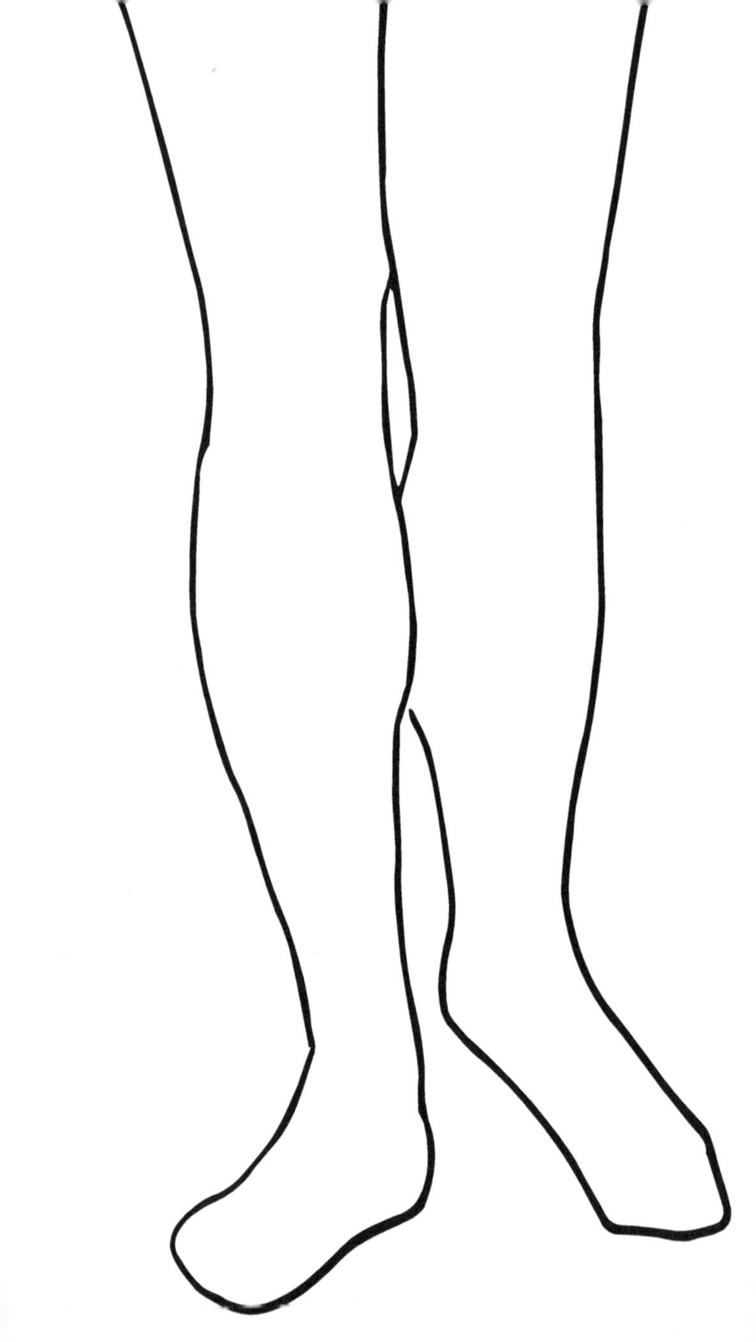